the elephant in the room

Designed by Bhairavi Patel

ISBN 978-1-937650-51-3
Library of Congress Control Number 2015936897

SMALL
BATCH
BOOKS

493 South Pleasant Street
Amherst, Massachusetts 01002
413.230.3943
smallbatchbooks.com

ACKNOWLEDGMENTS

Major funding for the publication of this book was provided by Oticon Corporation and the Vermont chapter of Hands & Voices. Thanks also to Tom Gilmartin and Lightspeed Technologies for their generous donation.

My sincere appreciation goes to Terry Keegan, co-ordinator for the Deaf and Hard of Hearing Program at Nine East Network, and William Gurney, former president of the Vermont Center for the Deaf and Hard of Hearing, for their support and encouragement during the development of this book.

—J. B.

THE elephant IN THE ROOM

By Jim Bombicino

Illustrated by Gildas Chatal

BUZZZZZZ.

BUZZZZZZZ.

FLASH.

FLASH.

The light-flashing alarm clock came to life, waking Skyler and his dog with a start. "Woof, woof!" barked Shadow, sounding his own alarm.

"OK, OK! I'm up . . . I'm up," croaked Skyler.

Skyler thought he heard a sound far off in the distance.

"I bet that's Mom calling.

UGH,
I DON'T FEEL MUCH LIKE
TALKING TODAY."

Skyler snatched his hearing aids from the nightstand and started to get dressed. As he did, he saw his little sister, Maizy, appear at the door.

"Why don't you feel like talking?" asked Maizy.

"BECAUSE IT'S

TOO HARD

TO LISTEN. . . even with my
hearing aids."

"Oooooh," said Maizy.

Skyler was HUNGRY. He went straight to the cupboard.

His big brother, Joe, was already at the table watching *Wake Up America!* Without looking up, he said, "Yo, Skyler. What's up, dude?"

For Skyler, what was up was his Cuckoo Crunchies.

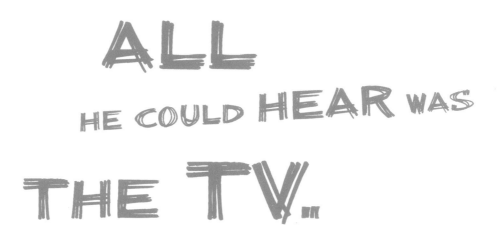

ALL HE COULD HEAR WAS THE TV.

Skyler turned from the cupboard. Joe was already on his way out the door. "Have a good one, squirt!"

SKYLER

MISSED

IT.

"You like my shirt?" he guessed.

Skyler switched off the TV and was just
about to pour cereal into his bowl, when in
came Sally from behind.

"GOOD
MOOOOORNING!"

SHE SANG.

SKYLER JUMPED,

and the Crunchies flew everywhere.

"Don't sneak up on me!" yelled Skyler.

"I wasn't sneaking! I was just being cheerful," said Sally.

"Well I'm not," said Skyler. "And

I DON'T FEEL LIKE TALKING."

"Well, do you feel like picking up cereal? 'Cause it's all over the floor," laughed Sally.

Skyler was mad. "Grrrrr," he growled.

Maizy growled too. "We're tigers!" she said.

Skyler finally collected his bowlful of cereal and sat down to eat. In came Dad. "Hey, there he is!

GOOD MORNING, SON."

"Morning, Dad."

Dad turned away to fix his morning coffee.

"So, Sky,

I'M STINKY

AND YOUR SOCKS ARE

TOO TIGHT."

"What?!" asked Skyler.

Turning around, Dad continued, "I'm really looking forward to watching you practice!"

Skyler was confused. "My socks fit OK," he said.

"Your socks? No, I said I'm picking you up at soccer tonight!"

Skyler was relieved. That was enough about socks and Dad being stinky. "Oh, well yeah, that would be good. I guess I didn't hear you right."

"THAT'S ALL RIGHT, SKY, DON'T YOU WORRY ABOUT IT.

I'll see you later on the field."

Skyler sighed.

Skyler finished his cereal and brought his bowl to the sink. Just as he did, in came his mom. She gave him a hug.

"Good morning, Skyler. I see you are up! Are you all right? You didn't answer me when I called up to you before."

"Oh, I'm fine. It's just that I was upstairs . . . and I don't feel much like talking today."

SKYLER DIDN'T FEEL MUCH LIKE EXPLAINING, EITHER.

Of course, Mom wanted to cheer him up.

"OH, SURE YOU DO. SALLY WOULD LOVE TO TALK TO YOU.

She's pretty excited about something today."

Sure enough, Sally was just about to burst into the room.

"Hey Skyler, guess what?!"

"No," replied Skyler.

"This is my new Farmer Jane doll. I'm bringing her to school for my presentation today."

"Lemme see! Lemme see!" interrupted Maizy.

Sally continued, "She's an organic farmer and she has all these garden tools, and—"

"Can I see? Can I see?" whined Maizy.

"WHOA! STOP!"

yelled Skyler.

"YOU'RE BOTH TALKING AT ONCE!"

"OK, OK, MR. GROUCH!

QUIET DOWN, MAIZY,"

said Sally as she scooped her up. "This is Farmer Jane. She's got a bunch of tools. I'm gonna use her to report on locavore farming for my science class!"

"Now, your turn," Sally said, as she released Maizy from her grasp.

"I HAVE MY OWN SPECIAL FRIEND TOO, SEE!"

said Maizy. She was very proud of her elephant.

Sally, in a hurry as usual, headed for the door. "AndImgonnadoasciencefairprojectongrowing-localproduceforthefarmersmarketand . . ."

Skyler's head was spinning. He thought he'd just heard the longest word in the world, but what was it?

"Huhhhh?" was all he could say.

"OH, NEVER MIND. IT DOESN'T MATTER,"

said Sally. And then she was gone.

Maizy had an idea. She walked over to Skyler and tapped his leg to get his attention.

Using her best speech, she said, "Sally's doing a science fair project. It's about Farmer Jane and her garden. Before you go to school, will you play tea party and talk with us?"

AND
FOR THE
FIRST TIME
THAT MORNING,

Skyler smiled.

Mom and Dad watched from the doorway as Skyler and Maizy had tea.

Mom whispered to Dad, "Look, honey. Skyler's happy to chat when he can understand more easily. Let's try to remember we should

GET CLOSE,
SPEAK CLEARLY,
AND BE
FACE TO FACE
WHEN WE TALK

to him. Listening is hard work for all of us, but especially when you have a hearing loss."

"Huh?" said Dad.

RESOURCES FOR INFORMATION ON HEARING LOSS

Alexander Graham Bell Association for the Deaf & Hard of Hearing: International non-profit membership organization, support network, and resource center on pediatric hearing loss and spoken language approaches and related issues. *agbell.org*

American Society for Deaf Children (ASDC): A national organization of families and professionals that helps create opportunities for children who are deaf and hard of hearing to gain full communication access, particularly through the use of sign language. *deafchildren.org*

American Speech-Language-Hearing Association (ASHA): Provides information for the public, professionals, and students about communication and communication disorders. *asha.org*

Central Institute for the Deaf: A unique network of resources on the progressive treatment of adult and childhood deafness. *cid.edu*

Hands & Voices: Nonprofit, parent-driven organization that provides support to families with children who are deaf or hard of hearing. *handsandvoices.org*

Laurent Clerc National Deaf Education Center: Provides information on various subjects related to deafness, including topics of interest to parents of children with hearing loss and multicultural issues. *clerccenter.gallaudet.edu/infotogo*

National Institutes of Health's (NIH) National Institute on Deafness and Other Communication Disorders (NIDCD): Federal government's focal point for biomedical and behavioral research in human communication. Website provides information about hearing, ear infections, and deafness. *nidcd.nih.gov*

Supporting Success for Children with Hearing Loss: A website to help professionals and family members of children who are hard of hearing or deaf improve their lives with resources, products, continuing education, and membership networking services. *successforkidswithhearingloss.com*

Author *JIM BOMBICINO* (above right) began his career as an audiol-ogist serving children in their classrooms at the Austine School for the Deaf. Af-ter becoming a school psychologist (and hearing-aid wearer himself), he started consulting and is now with Nine East Network in Montpelier, Vermont, serving deaf and hard-of-hearing students in a variety of educational settings. As a way to get his message across to early elementary school students, he wrote, pro-duced, and performed a puppet show highlighting "5 Ways to Say Good Day"– points to keep in mind when conversing with friends who have hearing loss. *The Elephant in the Room* is his latest effort to reach out to kids and their parents, this time with a colorful new picture book. Bombicino lives in southern Vermont with his wife, Jean, and Ruby, their "dog in the room."

Illustrator *GILDAS CHATAL* (above left) grew up in the area sur-rounding the city of Nantes in southern Brittany, France. Although deeply at-tached to this region, he went to study art in Paris, where he stayed to work as a graphic designer and illustrator. Drawing, painting, and illustrating have always been an essential part of his life. Chatal finds his inspiration mainly in nature. After eleven years in Paris, he moved to forested New England. Chatal lives in southern Vermont with his daughter, Maela.

Photo by Liz LaVorgna

CPSIA information can be obtained at www.ICGtesting.com
Printed in the USA
BVIW12n0010180117
473663BV00002B/1